# Pout-Pout Fish
# Special Valentine

Written by **Wes Adams**     Illustrated by **Isidre Monés**

Based on the *New York Times*–bestselling Pout-Pout Fish books
written by Deborah Diesen and illustrated by Dan Hanna

**Farrar Straus Giroux**
New York

Farrar Straus Giroux Books for Young Readers
An imprint of Macmillan Publishing Group, LLC
120 Broadway, New York, NY 10271

Color separations by Embassy Graphics
Printed in China by RR Donnelley Asia Printing Solutions Ltd., Dongguan City, Guangdong Province
Designed by Aram Kim
First edition, 2019
10 9 8 7 6 5 4 3 2 1

mackids.com

Library of Congress Control Number: 2019931330
ISBN: 978-0-374-31055-4

Our books may be purchased in bulk for promotional, educational, or business use.
Please contact your local bookseller or the Macmillan Corporate and Premium Sales Department at
(800) 221-7945 ext. 5442 or by email at MacmillanSpecialMarkets@macmillan.com.

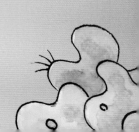

Mr. Fish was on his way home. He had been shopping for supplies to make Valentine's Day treats and cards for all his friends. His bags were heavy, and he was feeling tired.

He cheered up when he saw his octopus friend. "Have you been to the craft store, by any chance?" asked Mr. Eight. "I need something to add sparkle to my valentines."

Mr. Fish was pleased to share his glitter and glue with his friend.

He found Ms. Clam and Mrs. Squid in a fluster. They had been up all night making heart-shaped cookies—many, *many* cookies—and they had run out of ingredients for the icing!

Mr. Fish had just what they needed. He was glad to sweeten their day and lighten his load at the same time.

"Thank you, Pout-Pout Fish," said Mrs. Squid.
"You've made us both happy as clams!" said her baking partner.

Swimming up from the deep, deep dark, Mr. Lantern was searching for sea flowers for his valentines, but he wasn't having much luck.

"Why don't you make some?" asked Mr. Fish.
Mr. Lantern said he didn't know how.

From his bags, Mr. Fish took scissors, construction paper, and tape.
He showed Mr. Lantern how to make blooms of all shapes and sizes.

"These are perfect," said Mr. Lantern, glowing with pride.

When he got home, Mr. Fish was feeling better after helping his friends. But then he realized he'd used up most of the supplies he'd bought to make his own valentines.

He worried that his Valentine's Day plan would be ruined.

He decided to do the best he could with what he had—
a few sheets of paper and some colored pencils. As he worked
on his cards, he thought of a special message for each of his
pals, which he wrote with loving care.

When he was almost done, he saw a passing post-fish and gave her all the valentines to deliver...

Except for his last one. When it was ready, he decided to deliver it himself.

Miss Shimmer thought his homemade card was wonderful.
"Thank you!" she said. She gave him a valentine, too—
a box of candy.

While they shared the treats, Mr. Fish told her about his day.
"It sounds like you are everyone's special valentine," Miss Shimmer said.
"Oh, I don't know about that," Mr. Fish said.

But Miss Shimmer was right. While Mr. Fish was away from home, everyone got together to show their friend how much he meant to them.

Mr. Fish returned to find a Valentine's Day surprise waiting for him with a joyful message he would never forget.

HAPPY VALENTINE'S DAY, POUT-POUT FISH! WE LOVE YOU

Mr. Eight    Ms. Clam    Mrs. Squid    Mr. Lantern    Miss Shimmer

**Have a SPARKLY**
**Valentine's Day!**

**Happy**

**Valentine's Day!**

**Have a HAPPY**
**Valentine's Day!**

**Happy Valentine's Day!**